HIS GIRL

ARIA COLE

Hawk Larson left small-town Indiana to become one of the most famous quarterbacks on the planet, throwing winning passes for the Bears and living the dream. Life looked picture-perfect from the outside, but after five years, he still can't shake the memory of the one thing he left behind...the girl who owned his heart and crushed it one fateful night.

After an injury benches Hawk for good, he returns to the town he left, confronting the past and running headfirst into an unexpected future.

Life hasn't been easy in the five years since he left, and Morgan Quinn isn't the same girl she once was, her luscious hourglass curves and stubborn streak the only reminders of everything he left behind. She still rattles him to the core and leaves him craving more, but Morgan has a secret. A secret that may change the game for good.

Warning: When Hawk finally sees his Morgan again, he isn't sure if it's love or hate he's feeling, until fireworks fly at first touch and passion overcomes reason, leaving Hawk with the realization that he must protect his girl at all costs.

ONE

Morgan

"Look how high you are!"

Emerson shrieked as I gave her another push on the swing.

"Higher! I want to go as high as the clouds!"

"Not that high." I giggled at the sweet little four-year-old. "I might lose you way up there!"

"Higher! Higher!"

"No, it's time you come back down to earth. We should get back home for lunch."

"Can we have mac and cheese?" The swing slowed, and Emerson peered up at me with her big brown eyes. This little girl never failed to steal my heart.

"Anything you want, honey." I lifted her off the swing and looped our fingers, walking across the crisp green grass of the park. Emerson and I went to the park most days, mostly because it was only two blocks from our house.

"Can we go to the park after lunch too?"

"No, not today. I have to work for a few hours tonight. Mrs. Frisk is going to stay with you."

"But she smells like old hot dogs. And she always gives

me a goodnight kiss, and her breath smells."

I couldn't help the smile that turned my lips. The things that came out of this kid's mouth.

"Hey! Look at that doggy!" Emerson dropped my hand and darted off to a squatty little bulldog puppy, gnawing on the leash his owner held in one hand.

"Emerson!" I called, running after. "Ask if it's okay to pet the dog first!" My eyes landed on the owner of the dog just as I said the words.

And my heart stopped.

This couldn't be happening.

It wasn't possible.

Why was he back?

And what the hell do I say?

"Morgan?"

Shit. Too late.

"Hawk." I hadn't breathed that name in nearly half a decade. "Why are you here?"

His dark eyes fell on me, penetrating to my very soul, just like they always had.

My mind fell back to all the times we'd had together. The laughs, the touches, the first kiss, the first...

Hawk Larson was my first everything, and now he was standing right in front of me after all this time.

"Not exactly a nice way to welcome a guy home." His words were clipped, as if he were irritated by the very sight of me. Well, got news for you, buddy. Seeing you in my park isn't exactly what I would call a good day either.

"You're home?" I uttered, one hand reaching out for Emerson and pulling her to my side. I don't know why I felt the need to shield her because it only brought attention to her little cherubic face. The inquisitive eyes.

"I'm Emerson." She thrust out a hand. "What's your

name?"

Hawk's eyes held hers, oxygen sucked out of the air between the three of us. His eyes slid from hers to mine, narrowing with anger before landing on hers again. "I'm Hawk."

He shook her hand, and every cell in my body begged to disappear. Just melt into the dirt at my feet.

"Mommy is making mac and cheese for lunch. Do you like mac and cheese?" Her wide eyes were carefree and sparkling. I had to get us out of here. Standing toe to toe with Hawk left a pounding in my head, stole all the breath from my lungs, and damn that stubborn part of me that wanted to wrap him in a hug.

"I happen to love mac and cheese. It's nice to meet you, Emerson."

My gaze hung suspended on his, something in me urging me to pepper him with kisses just like I used to do when we were teenagers.

But those days were gone, and time had certainly changed both of us.

His broad shoulders, chiseled waist, the corded arms that had always danced just at the edges of my memory...but not even my memory could do him justice. I'd known him as a lean college quarterback, taut with sinewy muscle. The day he left for the NFL was the last time I'd seen him. For the first two years, Dad would turn on every game, beg me to watch with him, but I couldn't stand to see Hawk's face. Couldn't stand to see the happiness radiating across it. I knew this man. I'd known him from the time he was a boy throwing his first football. I'd cheered for him on the sidelines when he'd thrown the winning pass at homecoming. I'd been there with him through it all.

But not this.

Not now.

He was different.

Changed.

Older.

The jawline had grown sharper, now smattered with a dark five-o'clock shadow that had me itching to run my fingers across it.

Hawk's eyes trained on mine then, anger and confusion swirling.

"It was good to see you, *Morgan.*" He said my name like a curse word.

He still hated me.

Jesus, this couldn't be any worse.

Everything I'd done, I'd done for him. He was my heart—he always had been my heart. Why didn't he see that?

"Next time, ask your mom to add some bacon to the mac and cheese. Makes it ten times better." He winked at my daughter. Hawk Larson just winked at my daughter. *I can't believe this is happening.*

"Oh, she does! It's the bestest!"

Hawk's eyes cut into me, jaws crushed together. "She does, does she? Wonder where she learned that?"

"It's bacon, Hawk. It's not like you have a patent on bacon mac and cheese." I couldn't help the sarcasm. Why did it feel like five years had hardly passed and we were falling right back into old familiar habits?

"What's your dog's name?" Emerson bent to pet the puppy on the head again.

Hawk waited long moments before answering, bending down to place a hand on the dog's head and meet my daughter at eye level. "His name is Milo."

The air swooped from my lungs with that one word.

He'd named his dog after the kitten we'd found and raised together in high school?

The one my dad wouldn't let me keep, so Hawk had snuck it into his bedroom every night, hiding it under the covers while he slept. His mom had found out eventually and forced him to find a home for it. I'd cried like a baby the day we'd taken Milo to the farm outside of town to his new home. It was silly, we'd only had the kitten a few weeks, but I loved him. Somehow it felt like the first thing Hawk and I had together, a piece of both of us because we'd raised it. Hawk had held me in his arms, letting me cry out the tears.

Maybe I was preparing myself for him to leave then.

"You named him Milo?"

"Mommy used to have a cat named Milo!" Emerson smiled up innocently.

A tear burned behind my eyelid before I pulled her up to standing again. "We should get going, honey. I have to work tonight. Mrs. Frisk will be wondering where we are."

I stepped around Hawk, still hunched and petting his dog, eyes averted from mine.

So many words choking my throat.

Why hadn't he told me he was coming back?

Why hadn't I heard it before now? Usually, gossip tore around our little town like wildfire.

"Bye, Milo! Bye, Hawk!" Emerson waved enthusiastically as we walked away.

I could feel his eyes on us every step.

Every goddamn step, Hawk's eyes were on me, just like they always had been.

It used to make warmth curl up inside my belly. Hawk

took care of me like no one in my life ever had, which was why the anger he'd directed at me just now was like an iron dagger twisting in my back.

Hopefully, Hawk's visit to Greenville would be short-lived, then Emerson and my life could go back to normal. Hawk was anything but normal, and I'd loved him for it at one time. But now, every time I thought about him, my chest hurt like an oncoming heart attack.

I'd done my best to keep my head down and mind my own business the last five years, and that wasn't about to change, even if Hawk Larson was back in town.

TWO

Hawk

My head fucking pounded.

My chest ached.

My teeth goddamn hurt from clenching my jaw so much.

I really had to work at controlling my anger better. I rubbed a hand across my face as I finished walking Milo around the park.

Of all the people to run into my first week back in town, and it was her.

And she had a kid.

Morgan had a fucking kid, and that kid wasn't mine. I'd been gone for too long for that kid to be mine, and that meant she'd fucking cheated on me.

Well, it wasn't exactly cheating when she ripped my fucking heart out and left me bleeding on the floor.

No, that was a definite breakup.

But I guess, for me, it never had been. I'd been thinking about her nonstop. I couldn't get the soft touch of her lips against mine out of my head. The feel of her underneath me when I was sliding into her like a drug I was constantly chasing. The memory of the breathy sighs on her lips when I made her come. Morgan and I fit like puzzle pieces, a perfect set.

That was why I'd been so out of my mind when she'd left me.

I may have been the one to move out of state, but I would have married her, taken her with me, provided everything she needed. We could have lived the adventure together.

But instead, she told me she never wanted to see me again, and I believed her.

Instead of living life on the road with me, she stayed here, shacked up with someone else, and had the asshole's baby.

I hated her.

Nothing good could come out of seeing her again, and suddenly the decision to move back home after I permanently injured my rotator cuff seemed like the worst decision yet.

"Fuck, Milo, we should have run the other way when we saw her coming. Trouble. Women are nothing but trouble," I rambled to the pup. He turned, plopped on his ass, and hung his tongue out.

"Right. Glad we agree." I shook my head. "Let's go home, buddy. This has been too much crazy for one day."

He wagged his tail and jumped to his feet.

"I've got shit to do anyway. Those fan letters won't answer themselves, right?" I'd just received a huge box from my manager, fan mail, mostly from kids, that needed my reply. I had at least a few hours of signing photos and writing messages ahead of me.

I loved my fans; they're what kept me strong when two surgeries had failed to fix the problem. My pro career had been cut short, but truth be told, I was fine with that. Life on the road wasn't for me. I was a simple guy; I liked to be at home. Crowds and team trips weren't enjoyable. But I would always miss the fans. The look on the kids' faces when they looked up at you, believing all of their dreams could come true. Hell, mine had. Every single dream I had had become a reality, except for maybe the most important one. Her.

Morgan Quinn had been haunting me since the day I walked away.

***

I stretched my hands before placing the last personalized letter on the top of the stack. My stomach chose that moment to rumble. There wasn't an ounce of food in this house unless I wanted peanut butter and jelly again, which I didn't. This place was only temporary until my new house was move-in ready. Five bedrooms, six baths, a pool, and a gated yard. All the privacy I could ever want and room to expand long-term. Even when I'd left for the NFL, I'd known I would be back one day.

Greenville, Indiana had always been my home. The slower pace and quiet atmosphere called to me.

Playing pro for the Bears had been great, but I'd just been biding my time and saving my cash until I could move back home and buy a place big enough to live out the rest of my days in.

I glanced over at Milo, feet up and snuggled deep into the couch. "Guess you're not going anywhere."

I pulled my keys off the table, shoved them deep into my pocket, and then walked out the door.

A quick bite at the diner a few blocks away would have to do. I'd eaten enough pizza in the last week to kill a man, so something hot and homemade sounded about perfect.

The streetlights hummed as I walked through the darkness, hoping the diner was still open and wondering where in the hell I was going to start walking my dog to avoid Morgan's park.

Yeah, Morgan's park.

She could have it.

I'd take the dog to piss in the next county if that's what it took to avoid her and the sweet little face of her darling kid.

Just the thought alone made my stomach churn.

The nerve of her to slaughter my insides like that and then turn around and fuck someone else.

I hadn't been with another woman since her.

Not that I'd been saving myself, but the truth was, no one had ever compared.

No one had made me feel what Morgan made me feel. I'd held out for that, and I'd never found it.

A near growl escaped my lips as I thought about her touching someone else. Another man's paws on her soft skin. My skin. My girl. Mine.

I remembered the way she'd let me clutch her hand during my grandma's funeral, salty tears filling my eyes. Morgan had always been there for me, and then she'd gone and stolen my grandma's macaroni, cheese, and bacon recipe. So much for loyalty.

"Fuck, maybe I should sell the new place and move." I said the words out loud, swinging in the door of the diner as I did. "Fuck me."

There she was. Standing against the counter, back to

me.

I'd know that back anywhere.

The luscious curve of her hips, the hourglass waist, the way her ponytail hung over one shoulder.

She was so beautiful it hurt to look at her.

Without thinking twice, I strode right to her, my chest pressed against her back, my teeth at her ear. "What are you doing here?"

She spun, eyes wide as she was taken off guard. Her fiery greens narrowed before she spat, "I work here," and turned.

Fuck.

Fuck. Fuck. Double fuck.

"Of course you do." I couldn't help the growl.

"We're closing in thirty, but you're welcome to take a seat," she said simply, treating me like I was any other customer. The fuck I was any other customer. We had history. She couldn't just erase history.

I pushed a hand over my face and through my hair. "Where do you live?"

"Why would I tell you?" she shot back, a hand at her hip.

Another groan rolled through me. "Fine. I don't give a shit anyway."

"Then why ask?" Her eyes sparkled. She had me on that one. I did care. I cared a fuck of a lot. I didn't know why I cared, but I did.

"Because…" I paused, eyes locked on hers. The air hung heavy between us, her eyes searching mine, my gaze climbing up and down hers. Fuck, I wanted to pull her into my arms, kiss her until she couldn't fucking breathe and forgot every other man that had come since me. "Because I give a fuck about that little girl."

Her dark eyes grew wide, a look of stone-cold fear flashing across her face. What the hell was that about? And come to think of it, why had she looked like she'd seen a ghost when we'd met in the park? Introducing me to her daughter...

Shit.

Oh Jesus Christ.

Was it possible?

Could little Emerson actually be my daughter?

The thought hadn't even occurred to me before now. Dammit, had she found out she was pregnant after I left?

Suddenly, all the dark nights alone in my bed came back to me, my thumb hovering over her name in my contact list, memories of us dragging me under.

"Look, Hawk, I'm not sure why you came back, or why you're even standing here in front of me with that look on your face, but I'm fine. *We're* fine." She amended, referring to herself and Emerson and averting her eyes. "Now can I get you a drink?"

She twisted, turning her back on me, hands scribbling something on a pad she'd pulled out of her apron.

"Grrrr..." I gritted out, spinning on my heel and stomping out of the diner.

The cool air hit my face, clearing my head.

Fuck.

I couldn't leave her like that.

What if that little girl was mine?

And why did it feel like her mama still was, even after all these years?

I turned around, barging back through the doors and up to her, fists clenching at my sides, unsure of what to say.

So I didn't say anything.

13

I thrust my hands in her hair, threaded my fingers through the silky strands and smashed my lips to hers in a take-no-prisoners kiss. Her lips opened as if on instinct, just like they always had, and our tongues slipped together. Fireworks exploded between us, heart pounding within me, telling me to take what was mine.

Her hands worked into my hair, hips grinding against mine and driving me nearly blind with lust.

I needed her.

I wanted her.

I loved her.

Fuck.

I still loved her.

She pulled her lips from mine, small gasps breathing past her lips when my hands tightened at her cheeks. My eyes hardened, searching her up and down for the girl I used to know. Discovering the woman she'd become.

She was so lovely it made my chest ache.

"Jesus," I grunted, then spun, storming back out the doors and into the cool night. I walked a few steps, hands in my hair, mind raging at me to turn around and tell her she belonged to me. She'd always belonged to me. There was no severing what we had. What we had grew stronger, grew more alive.

Fuck, I had to say something.

I couldn't just turn tail and run like a bitch. I couldn't stand here with my hands in my hair.

I whirled around, throwing the door open and bursting through again. Walking straight for her, and this time, she didn't turn when I neared. This time, she stood her ground, eyes watching me intently. She was bold, brave. She'd been through alot in the years since I'd left her.

And it only registered just then that if she was working at the diner, she was probably struggling to make ends meet. She was probably a single mom. No man in his right mind would let his woman work somewhere like this at night, with all the fucking assholes that came into places like this after dark.

"I don't know what to do about you," I breathed, lips barely brushing hers.

Fuck, I wanted her plastered to me again.

I wanted her home, in bed, screaming my name. I wanted everything with this woman.

But that didn't change the fact that she'd still left me. Told me she never wanted to see me again and then walked away, told me to leave and never come back.

Christ, I'd begged her to come with me.

I told her I would stay, forget the NFL, all I wanted was her.

But she insisted.

And now, looking across at her, eyes connecting, shared memories swirling, I couldn't help the pain clogging my heart.

"Just leave, Hawk," she finally whispered, eyes turning down.

I caught her chin, forcing her to look at me. "Got news for you, Morgan. I'm never leaving again."

THREE

Morgan

His words echoed around my skull.

Never? Did he really mean never?

"I thought you were just here for a break. Don't you have a big fancy career to get back to?"

His eyes softened for a minute, his hand falling from my chin and leaving tingles in its wake. Everything about him turned me on, still did. Only now, I hated him for it. "Not going back."

"Ever?"

He only shook his head. As if he didn't owe me more of an explanation. Of course, he owed me an explanation. This was *my* town; he'd up and left us all. I was the one who was left behind to make a life here.

"Fucked up my shoulder." He rubbed at the muscle, and my instincts pushed at me to touch him. Massage him. Ease away the ache. But those days were gone. I wasn't his anymore, and he certainly wasn't mine. "I'm officially retired."

"Shit." I blurted the only word in my head.

"Something like that," he muttered, eyes trailing around the small diner.

It wasn't much to look at, the floors dingy, the seat cushions cracked, but Dan had been good to me. Always flexible with hours, understanding when Emerson was sick. And this was just about the only place to work in this town. Anything else would require driving into the city, a good forty-five minutes, and doing that every day with my junk car would be bad news.

We were okay. I could make rent on the wage Dan paid, and if I picked up additional hours, I had enough to buy extras at the grocery store, like ice cream for a treat, or a new pair of sandals for Emerson in the summer.

Life was tough, and looking at Hawk now, I could see he'd left this life far behind.

His shoes were high-end sneakers, brand-new jeans hung just right on his hips, and he wore a designer T-shirt I was sure he paid more for than what I spent a month in groceries. Hawk and I may have grown up together, but our lives sure were different now. His dad had always said I wasn't good enough for him, and it was part of the reason I'd told Hawk to walk away—because it was true. I couldn't hold him back when his only dream had ever been to play pro ball. I wouldn't be the weight on the end of his balloon. Hawk deserved to fly. He was the best quarterback Greenville had seen in over a decade. Of course, he was drafted his sophomore year of college, and no way would I be the girl to keep him from chasing his dreams.

I loved him enough for that, at least.

Even if he didn't see it, standing across from me now.

"Talk to me. Just fifteen minutes," Hawk breathed against my neck.

Dan's voice called from the back of the kitchen then,

asking me to lock the doors.

"I'll wait for you outside. Please talk to me." Hawk's eyes burned back at me, dark, pleading.

I nodded quickly, ushering him out the door before locking it behind him. He turned, waved once, then leaned against the brick wall, looking sexy as fuck. How was it possible Hawk was back and he was waiting for me to get off work, just like it used to be? I'd fallen into a time warp, except this time, it was all different. This time, I had Emerson.

I breathed deeply, steeling my spine before buzzing around to the tables and counters and giving them one final sweep with a damp cloth. Untying my apron, I went in back to find Dan.

"Headed home for the night?" He barely looked up from the stack of papers on his desk.

"Yup, unless you need anything else?" I stalled, dreading walking out those doors to face Hawk. Who knew what kinds of questions he might ask me. And I wasn't ready to tell him anything. Not yet, maybe not ever.

"I'm good. Thanks, Morgan." Dan dismissed me with a wave of his hand, and I trailed on soft footsteps out the back door. Shrugging my purse onto my shoulder, I made my way around the building and bumped chest-first into Hawk.

His arms came around me instantly.

My body wanted to melt into him, let him soothe away all the anxiety just like he used to do, but I'd gotten good at standing on my own two feet. Just because he was back now didn't change anything.

"What do you want, Hawk?"

"I want to know about you," he said simply. I'd missed

that about him. So many people used so many words to fill their conversations without saying anything of value. Hawk's words were short and to the point, and you never had to guess how he was feeling.

"Well, I've been waitressing here for almost three years —"

"Not that shit."

I frowned, growing frustrated. "Then, what shit?"

"Don't bullshit me, Morgan." He caught my elbow, hauling me a little closer to him. My stomach fell, my knees weakened, stubborn arousal chugging its way through my veins and landing between my thighs. Just the brush of his skin against mine was like a hit of heroin coursing through my veins. I hated being so at his mercy. I hated that he still knew that about me.

"Bullshit you? Why would I even?" I yanked my arm out of his grip and walked down the sidewalk.

"Talk to me."

"You keep saying that without asking a damn question!" I screamed, speeding up.

"Christ, can't we go somewhere private?" His face contorted into a frown.

"No! I mean, not my place. The babysitter is there."

"Then mine." His hand was at my elbow again, pulling me against him.

I shook my head, not because I didn't want to, but because the fog his touch sent clouding my brain was almost too much to handle.

"It's just a block and a half away. Give me fifteen minutes. And I'll walk you home when I'm done."

"I don't want you to know where I live."

"What? Why not?" His brow furrowed, offended.

I shook my head, feeling a little more helpless every

minute. I wasn't sure what I was doing here, the only thing running through my head that I was standing across from my best friend, and following him anywhere felt like the most natural thing on Earth. I sighed, "Fifteen minutes at your place. That's it."

He shook his head, hand looping with mine as he guided us the opposite way down the street. His fingers intertwined with mine made my stomach swim, my knees weak, the taste of his lips on mine still intoxicating.

Hawk took another turn down a side street, weaving farther away from my and Emerson's house—at least he wasn't my neighbor. Small mercies for that.

My heart stuttered to a halt when we approached a small, very familiar apartment complex. The very same apartment complex we'd lived in together for the first two years of college.

The two years before he left.

The two years before my entire world changed.

"You live here?" I asked in disbelief.

He only nodded, hand firmer in mine as we walked across the parking lot. He pulled a key out of his pocket and unlocked a door on the bottom floor. "Only temporary. Got a place outside of town. This place had good memories, though." He looked at me, a half grin turning his lips.

That grin.

Jesus, how could I have forgotten that grin?

It sent cartwheels flipping in my stomach every time.

What was I doing here?

I should have gone straight home.

"Seeing you today made me realize something, Morgan. Something that's been buried a long time." He was moving closer, his other hand catching mine. "I may have walked away from you then, but you're just as much mine now as you were all those years ago." His words crept up the curve of my neck, teeth nipping at my earlobe.

Oh. God. Yes.

"I shouldn't have left you here. I should have dragged you kicking and screaming along with me."

A part of me wished he would have.

"Or I should have stayed, Morgan. Fuck, every day I kicked myself for not staying."

"W-what?" I stammered, brain fried with the way his hands were crawling up my waist, slipping under my shirt and making me putty in his hands.

"I never stopped loving you, Morgan. Not a day went by that I didn't love you."

His words sucked the air from the room.

My vision darkened, my muscles weak before his hands were at my hips and pulling me against him.

He hitched my legs around his waist. His hands were forcing their way into my hair, ripping out my ponytail and sending my hair in a cascade around us. Heaving pants of desperate breath racked us both as our lips attached, our sanity gone, our love beating stronger than it ever had.

I hated him.

I loved him.

I needed him.

I needed this.

"Oh, Hawk," I sighed when his hand slipped under my skirt, fingers working against the fabric of my panties. I was aching, desperate, hungry for his body against mine.

"Missed you, baby girl," were the last words he said

before his fingers slipped inside my panties and his lips covered my moans.

I was lost.

Hawk was back, and I'd already fallen down the rabbit hole.

FOUR

Hawk

She careened against me as I launched us down the hallway, her legs wrapped around my waist just like I'd been dreaming of all those nights, all those years.

"Never thought I'd have you in my arms again," I growled at her ear before kicking my door closed and pushing her against it. "Never thought I'd have my hands on your skin again. My lips on your body, my tongue tasting every inch of you."

Her breath came out in ragged gasps, the pulse hammering at her throat matching mine.

I pushed her arms above her head, locking them with my hand, and trailed a nose down the inside of her arm. She shivered, gasping for air, her hips grinding against my cock like she was begging for it.

"Tell me, tell me how much you fucking missed this cock inside you."

She grunted, eyes slammed closed as her tits heaved in my face.

I latched on to the outline of one nipple, sucking and nipping, making her hum with pain before letting go.

"Say it. I want to hear you say how many nights you

dreamed about my cock slipping inside you, taking your breath away, making you beg for more."

"Yes… Fuck, yes… Is that what you want to hear? Yes, I dreamed about you, Hawk. I dreamed about this." She hummed, eyes still averted.

Fuck that.

"I need your eyes on me for this, baby girl." I tipped her chin to mine, her eyes slamming open. "Daddy's here now. I'm here, and I've got you," I groaned at her ear, holding her chin in my hand. My cock dug into her stomach, aching for the searing hot feel of her pussy. "I never forgot this."

My lips covered hers in a kiss that branded. A kiss that showed her that I still owned this, I owned her—and every pleasurable sigh she ever had or ever would have.

"We're not young anymore, Morgan. I was a boy then, but I'm a man now. I know what I want, and there's only ever been one thing."

Her eyes trained on mine, her teeth clamping down onto her lip when I shoved the skirt over her hips.

"I couldn't see a single day without you in it. All those people calling my name, telling me they loved me, but the only person's love I've ever cared about getting is yours," I hissed at her ear. "And you crushed it."

Her gorgeous, haunted eyes flickered with pain, but I didn't care. I didn't give a fuck, because I'd spent one too many nights of the last five fucking years thinking about her, this moment, us. Always us.

"You destroyed me," I breathed, tearing her panties down her thighs and pulling them to shreds in my hands.

I pulled the zipper down on my jeans a moment later and freed my cock, my only thought getting lost inside her again. Just one more time. Chase the pain away with my favorite drug.

"You broke my heart, Hawk," she said just as my cock slid past her soaked entrance.

My hands clutched her hips, my lips at her neck sucking, drawing blood to the surface, desperate to make her feel what she'd made me feel.

"I hate that I need you," I gasped, finally seated fully inside her. Her warm pussy fluttered around me, waves of pleasure rolling through us as our bodies melded for the first time in too long.

"It's like you never left." She whimpered, her fingernails digging into my shoulder blades.

I pushed a hand through her hair, whispering, "Daddy's here now. You're going to be okay. I'm here to take care of you, baby girl."

I fucked her slowly, dragging in and out until every nerve was raw, every inch between us laid bare. Naked. Just like we were meant to be.

My hands cupped at her backside, my teeth nibbling at her throat as I dragged us to the bed, pushing her down beneath me and caging her in. Slipping the shirt off her shoulders, I groaned when she writhed and moaned.

The years looked good on her. She'd been gorgeous then, but she'd filled out. I imagined motherhood did that, and I instantly regretted that I hadn't been here to see her become a mother. See her body round and beautiful with child, growing and changing, her curves developing as she grew into a mother.

"So fucking beautiful. Christ, I missed this. Tell Daddy where you want him to kiss you," I urged before I could think about the words. Her hands gripped the hard muscle of my back, nails digging into my flesh and driving me wild with pleasure.

"My nipples. Oh my God, your lips on my nipples."

I sucked on the sharp little peaks, plucking at the tender flesh with my teeth and earning more moans and arches from her.

It had always been like this with us.

From the beginning, Morgan had liked our fucking raw, uninhibited. And the way she was grasping at me now made me think she hadn't had this in a long time.

About as long as I had.

"I can't stand to think of another man's hands on your skin. Covering your body. Kissing your lips. *My* lips." I thrust my tongue past her mouth, twisting our tongues and showing her instead of telling her just how I felt.

I was mad.

Angrier than hell.

But underneath all that, I missed her.

Fuck, I'd missed her too goddamn much.

And now here she was, underneath me, soft and open, welcoming me into her body, when what I really needed was her heart.

"Fuck," I moaned, adding my thumb, whispering over the aroused bud of her clit before I pushed harder, pinched, and soothed away the pain. Ground my hips against her body, made her really feel what she did to me. "You make me so hard, Morgan. You feel what you do to me? That's all for you. One look in your pretty eyes at the park, and I nearly lost it. You've always been mine, Morgan. I may have been stupid enough to let you go then, but not anymore."

I flipped her in my hands, shoving into her from behind, holding her against my chest as I kneaded her gorgeous tits in my palms.

"I've been fucking starved." I nipped at her earlobe, sliding a hand between her thigh and running fast circles around her pussy until she was shaking around my dick.

I may only have one night with her. This girl was good at leaving, and that realization was like an ax to my heart. I didn't know if I could take her leaving again.

I turned her around in my arms again, forcing her to face me, forcing our lips to connect.

"I hate that I love you." The words came out ragged against her lips.

She sucked in a breath of air when I shoved into her again, my hips thrusting so quickly this almost felt like a punishment fuck. Almost.

I'd craved this, pushed it aside for far too long while I focused on the game and my future. But this, right here, was where I came the most alive. Buried inside Morgan was the only place I ever needed to be.

"Oh God, Hawk. Hawk!" she sang, pussy quivering around me as another orgasm barreled through her body.

"God, yes, baby girl. So responsive. Daddy missed that about you." I sucked at her lips, swallowing her sighs, consuming her whole. "Tell me no one else has done what I do to you. Has made you feel how this fat cock makes you feel," I ordered, my cock pulsing harder, angrier, closer to the edge.

"No!" she whispered, breathless. "No, no, no one," she cried, chest still heaving with ragged pants.

I covered her pert nipple with my lips, sucking it into my mouth as I ground my hips against her, bottoming out, filling her up, giving her every long, hard inch of me. I wanted her claimed. I wanted to coat her with my come and send her off down the street, a warning to any man to stay ten feet away. I'd yank the eyeballs from any man who so much as looked at her the wrong way. Morgan brought out every protective instinct in me, a drive that only came out with her.

"Good. Makes me happy to know this is still mine." I pulled my cock from her hot body, jerking my dick until long, hot streams of come splashed across her creamy abdomen. I stood over her, marking her, leaving my brand, the orgasm chasing through me the most powerful I'd ever felt.

"You dirty girl, look how hungry your pretty pink pussy is." I slipped my hands through her hot folds, then slid our juice across her creamy skin. Around her navel, up her stomach, and over her gorgeous, heavy tits. "You like exposing yourself to me? Showing me that hard little clit. God, I love your pussy so much. Daddy's property."

Her eyes held mine for long, quiet beats before she made to roll out of bed.

"No fucking way you're leaving yet." I caught her wrist.

"I have to. I'm sorry," she said softly. I cursed the dark shadows in my room, hiding her from my greedy eyes.

"Okay, I'll walk you." I hopped out of bed, handing her the clothing I'd torn off her as we'd tumbled through the apartment.

"I'm okay." She took her bra from me. "Really." She slid her panties up her thighs.

"Wish I could kidnap you, baby girl." I meant it. I meant those words more than I'd ever meant anything. I meant it then, and I sure as hell meant it now.

"I don't need saving, Hawk. I know that's always been your thing, but I've done perfectly fine on my own."

"I can tell," I huffed before I could catch myself.

"What does that mean?" She turned on me, hand on her hip, the silver light of the moon sliding across her body. I hated that she was getting dressed, not undressing and falling into my bed all over again. This reunion was ending far too soon. I hadn't wasted half a decade for thirty minutes.

"It means I can help you. I can be there—for *both* of you."

Her eyes hardened. "I don't need that."

She pulled her skirt up her legs, then shoved on her shirt. Her apron was stuffed into the back pocket of her skirt a moment later, and then she was hustling out the door like she couldn't leave fast enough.

"Morgan!" I called, pulling my own shirt over my head and following her out.

I reached for her hand when I caught up, but she kept walking.

"I mean it. I don't need your help, Hawk. I don't need anything from you. Not a goddamn thing." She broke out of my grasp and continued walking down the sidewalk.

"Dammit, Morgan, we have to talk!"

"Oh, that's rich coming from you," she spat, yanking out of my hold again and turning down a side street.

"Jesus, I'm going to need to start training every day again if I'm going to keep up with you."

Her hand thrust behind her, middle finger in the air, long hair flowing in a curtain around her. A hint of that sarcastic smile I loved so much darted across her lips before she schooled her expression again.

She was still the girl I knew, the girl I loved.

"First, you steal Gram's mac and cheese recipe, then you flip me the bird? On fire, aren't ya?" I shot back.

"Christ, Morgan, just give me a minute." I finally caught her.

"I gave you a lot just now, and still, you managed to insult me." She shook her head, jaw clenching and unclenching.

"Fuck, you're right." I pushed a hand through my hair. "I'm sorry. I've been driving myself insane…" I looked up at the stars sprinkled in the inky sky, one thought chugging through my brain on repeat. "I was a fucking dumbass not to think of it the moment I saw you…and her… Morgan." I caught her gaze, voice lowering another octave as emotion clogged my throat. "Is she mine?"

FIVE

Morgan

Angry tears pricked behind my eyelids as I thought about all the time that'd gone by.

I didn't owe him an explanation. He didn't even deserve to come along one day and ask me this question.

If he'd really cared, wouldn't he have been back the first month? Calling the first week? Writing letters? Anything?

The truth was, he'd done nothing.

Absolutely nothing. Just walked away and forgot about the life he'd made here.

Had I asked him to do that? Sure. Does that mean he should have?

No. God, no.

So I didn't feel like I owed him that answer. But then our eyes caught, unspoken words hanging heavy between us.

Memories. Emotions. Love.

I hated that I still loved him too.

I hated him and I loved him, and those were two completely different emotions waging a brutal war in my gut.

But in the end, the girl that loved him won out.

The girl that remembered the way he used to catch me when I fell made the decision.

"Come inside?" I asked, catching his hand with mine, the first tender moment I'd felt toward him in so long. Earlier we'd fucked, but this, this was penetrating my soul on another level. This deserved more, and so did he.

I owed him more.

"In?" he asked, hand covering mine in that old familiar way it used to.

"This is my place." I nodded behind me, an old Victorian walk-up, dilapidated shutters and rotten railings greeting his gaze.

"What about…?"

"It's fine." I shrugged it off. "Mrs. Frisk won't mind. I'm a grown woman."

I walked ahead of him up the stairs, never imagining we'd have this moment together. Never imagining I would ever see him again, much less welcome him into my home. Into my family.

"Em's been asleep for over an hour, and I left some fried chicken in the fridge for you— Oh." Mrs. Frisk paused when her eyes landed on me and then my visitor. "Hawk? Is that you?"

"Sure is, ma'am."

"Good God, it's been a while." She placed a kiss on his cheek. "Just visiting before you're back to the city?"

"No, ma'am. Here to stay. Bought a house outside of the town line."

"Oh." Mrs. Frisk looked from me to Hawk, then made a big show of gathering up her purse and knitting and scuttling out the door. "I'll leave you two alone, then."

"Thank you, Mrs. Frisk." I winked at her, closing the

door as she descended the steps.

"She hasn't changed a bit, still matchmaking and gossiping."

"Same as ever." I paused, taking him in. He was gorgeous, still young, still so…unlike me. Was he unlike me? Had we drifted too far apart? I was a mom now, and that would forever and always come first. Was he ready for that?

I couldn't think of a thing to say to him. So instead, I pulled out the photo album from the rickety bookshelf, the one stuffed full of all of Emerson's firsts. First smile, first step, first haircut—it was her life, condensed into a book of shiny pages.

I sat down on the couch, patting the seat next to me, and placed the book in his lap once he sat. "First, please know that I never thought I would see you again."

His eyes hardened in the dim light, hand moving mine away so he could open the book.

Emerson Riley Larson – Born August 21

Hawk gnashed down on his teeth, eyes trailing over the words again and again.

"Larson?" he finally breathed.

I nodded, unable to keep the lump from forming in my throat.

"She's mine? That little girl in there is mine, and you never told me? She has my last name, and yet she doesn't even call me Dad?" He stared me down.

My stomach turned to acid, the urge to throw up powerful. "I didn't know what to do. I knew I couldn't ruin your life, Hawk. I knew the only dream you had was to get out of this town and play pro ball. I couldn't let us stop you."

"Us? Us. Jesus, Morgan, you knew? You knew you

33

were pregnant when you broke up with me?" The hard edge to his words turned my heart to ice.

"Y-yes, but—"

His face twisted then, that charming grin I loved long gone in favor of an angry scowl, something so dark I'd never seen in him before. "You destroyed me!" He shot to his feet. "You were my entire heart! And then you broke it. You broke me, and now you tell me you fucking lied? You kept my baby from me? A child who has my blood running through her veins? My last name?"

I followed him as he stalked out the door and onto the porch. Hands thrust in his hair, he paced up and down my yard, only grunts and huffs coming from his mouth. "I tried to do what was best. I loved you, I couldn't hold you back."

He turned then, striding toward me before stopping at my feet and plunging his hands into my hair, eyes steering mine as he growled. "That wasn't for you to decide."

My heart beat painfully against my ribs. "I loved you too much to stop you."

"You let me think we were over. That I'd ruined your life. That you hated me." His eyes were tortured.

"I had to, or you wouldn't leave!" I finally succumbed to the pain throbbing in my heart and fell to my knees. I pushed my hands into my hair and sobbed. "I'm so sorry. I thought I was doing the right thing, and now… I don't know. I don't know."

He dropped to his knees beside me, hands holding my cheeks and pulling my gaze to meet his.

"I was never good enough for you, Hawk. You came from something, you are going places. A girl like me only holds a guy like you back, and I couldn't live with myself if I'd—"

"Shut up. Fuck, woman, please just shut up." He covered my lips in a soft kiss. Kissing me slowly, he slid his tongue in and out, tasting me like he was savoring me. "I don't know what the fuck I'm going to do with you," he murmured, nose circling the shell of my ear. "But I want to get to know my daughter."

I hunched there stock-still, frozen in his arms as the realization there was no going back took over me.

Hawk knew now.

Hawk knew Emerson was his, and now I would have to split custody, share my daughter, make decisions for her with him.

With him.

Oh God, what had I done?

SIX

Hawk

She was mine.

I couldn't fucking believe it. After all these years, all this time, my girl had a little girl, *my* little girl.

"We're gonna have to get your stuff moved out of here tomorrow," I muttered, brain suddenly swirling with all the shit I had to do.

"Excuse me, what?" She looked up at me, eyes still wet with salty tears.

"Not leaving you and my little girl in this place. Not when there's something I can do about it."

"Hawk, we don't need you to do anything. Between my mom and Mrs. Frisk and me, we're getting along just fine with Emerson."

"My girl deserves a fuck of a lot more than just fine." I cupped her cheek, smoothing the pad of my thumb across her cheek. "Both of my girls do."

She tightened her jaw, standing up and brushing herself off. "Listen, Hawk Larson, I don't need your handout. I don't need anything from you."

"You need a daddy for that little girl," I said plainly.

The words must have hit their mark because Morgan

narrowed her eyes. "Don't start. You can see Emerson. You're welcome to come over for dinners and school functions, but—"

"But my ass, Morgan." I pulled her close to me, chest to chest, breath to breath. "I want all the fucking dinners with that little girl, and I want them with you too. Don't bother tellin' me you mind sharing a dinner with me because the way you just screamed my name back at my place proves otherwise. I can still make you come, Morgan. My skin against yours makes you mine. This —" I hammered my cock against her pelvis, making sure she felt every hard inch "—this belongs to you."

"Hawk..." She sucked in a breath, head landing against my chest as her body relaxed against mine.

"I'm here, baby, and I'm not leaving. God himself couldn't keep me away now."

Tears welled in her eyes, but I was determined to make this a good moment. I licked her tearstained cheeks, swallowing the pain, dragging her down to the grass with me. Kissing her was like being teenagers again, my hands crawling up her shirt, her luscious body grinding out a rhythm against mine. Cloaked in darkness, surrounded by the scent of lilacs and my girl, I came alive again.

"Come inside," she whispered.

"Been waiting for those words for too fucking long." I snaked my arms around her waist and hauled her against me, pounding up the rickety steps and through the door of her home.

"Can't wait to show you our new house."

"Our new house? You're a dog with a bone about this, aren't you?"

"About taking care of what's mine? Fuck yeah, I am."

I pushed her through the door of her bedroom after she pointed the way. Our lips clung together the entire time as we crashed into her room, silver moonlight careening across her bed, her hair, her body, making her look good enough to eat.

"You're a fucking angel, precious. You've grown into a woman," I murmured, lifting the shirt over her head and then unclasping her bra. Her heavy tits fell free, and I caught them with my palms, sucking and biting at the nipples until they were pink and hard.

Soft sighs slipped past her lips as her hands pushed into my hair, her legs naked and cradling my waist.

I nestled my cock between her thighs, rubbing against the hot, slick heat of her pussy.

My fucking heaven and my hell.

The very thing I'd drowned in, the thing I couldn't live without.

We were connected, Morgan and I. Had been from the start, even all those years ago when we shared our first kiss under the oak tree in my parents' yard.

That tree was still there.

Maybe I would marry her under that tree someday.

She groaned when my cock filled her, my fingers working at her back entrance as I whispered in her ear. "Missed you so much, baby. Can't even tell you how much."

"There was a time I didn't think I could live without you, Hawk," she said softly.

"Never have to worry about that again. Marrying you, baby girl. Going to make you my wife, move you and my little girl home, where you both belong. With me." Her nails bit into my back, and my fingers sped between her legs as an orgasm rushed through her.

"Fuck, baby." I kissed her, pumping harder, faster, chasing dreams I hadn't dared to dream in too fucking long.

"Love you more than I ever have." I sucked in a breath, my muscles burning as an orgasm rained down on me. Like a wave crashing, I pumped everything I had into my perfect, beautiful girl, getting lost in all the love we always created together.

We were still creating.

"Guess it's a little late to ask if you're on the pill or anything." I grinned, curling her into my body and tucking us both under the covers of her double bed.

"Well…" She averted her eyes. "I'm not on anything. I didn't think there was a reason for it. I haven't been with anyone since—"

"Since…?" I growled.

"Since you. You're the last person I was with, Hawk."

"Good. Hate to break any filthy bastard's fingers that put his hands on you."

"Well, I guess it's a good thing I saved my virtue, then."

"Hell, Morgan. I saw you and Emerson at the park, and I lost my mind. All I could think was that you'd been with someone else."

"Never. No one was…" She smiled softly. "No one was like you."

I sucked in a deep breath of air, pulling her closer, enjoying the sound of her soft breaths against my chest again. Hell, I think that's what I'd missed most, having her with me at night to hold on to. Waking up to face every morning with her.

Every hour in between.

"Morgan?" I began, tracing a fingertip around the

dimple of her navel.

"Yeah?" She yawned.

"Love you and Emerson more than my life. You're mine now."

"Mmm," she breathed, tucking closer under my shoulder. "Yours, Hawk."

EPILOGUE

Morgan - one year later

"Fuck, baby, every day you taste sweeter." Hawk's tongue was sliding between my wet folds.

He pushed the mountain of taffeta up with one hand, the other clutching at my hip as my ankles locked around his neck. "Oh God, Hawk!"

His teeth dragged across every raw nerve of my swollen clit, my muscles spasming as an orgasm fluttered through my system. My heart hammering, my legs lax around his shoulders, he hoisted me into his arms and laid us both back on the small double bed in his parents' guest bedroom.

The one they'd given me to get ready before Hawk and I walked down the aisle in just a few moments.

"That was amazing."

"That was just a teaser. I can't wait to rip this dress off you later." His crooked grin sent lightning bolts across my skin.

"You're going to have to wait at least a few hours. We have pictures, then the reception…"

"No way I'm waiting that long to fuck my beautiful new wife."

I erupted into giggles when his hands slid under my dress again, kneading at my inner thighs. The thick erection tenting his tuxedo pants made my mouth water. Would it be so wrong to suck him off five minutes before we walked down the aisle? I didn't think so.

Just then, a pounding sounded at the door.

"Shit," I breathed. "Busted."

Hawk chuckled before standing, adjusting his cock, and then doing a once-over of me. "Ready, my new bride?"

"Ready for forever with you?" I squinted up at him with a coy smile. "Absolutely."

He grinned, looping my hand with his and placing a kiss across my knuckles, the sparkling three-carat diamond glistening on my ring ringer.

He'd proposed just a few months after we'd met again, but there'd been another surprise waiting for us that delayed the wedding.

"Morgan?" My mother's voice called through the door, slightly shrill.

"Coming, Mom!" I winked at Hawk. He grinned, then swung the door wide open.

"Hawk! You're not supposed to see her—"

"Just couldn't help myself, ma'am." Hawk winked at my mom then lifted our six-week-old son from her arms. "Hey, little man, ready to watch Momma finally say 'I do' to your old man?"

I grinned, happy tears already wetting my eyes.

My life was perfect. Hawk had charmed his way back into my life, and he'd made my mother fall in love with him all over again too. The look on her face right now proved it.

"Give me my grandbaby, and you get out there. Your

dad's been looking everywhere for you." She swatted at Hawk's shoulder.

He did what she said, placing one more kiss on my knuckles before sauntering off down the hallway and out to the garden.

"I don't know what you were thinking, signing up for a lifetime with that one."

"I wasn't thinking." I smiled down at Noah, placing a kiss on his soft cheeks. "I was only feeling, Mama. And a lifetime without that man felt like a life not worth living."

She smiled, eyes warm with understanding. "He told me last night that you'd never have to work again, Morgan. That he'd take care of you for the rest of your life and your children's lives and your grandchildren's lives. Said he'd made enough while he was away to give you all that, at least." She paused, hand clutching mine. "He's a good man, that Hawk Larson. I never doubted him or your love for him. I always hoped we'd end up here."

I swiped at a tear. "Thank you, Mama. I couldn't have survived the last five years without you."

"You would have survived just fine, sweetheart. That's what women do, they survive every day. Now don't ruin your makeup. We've got a wedding to get to." She tsked, wiping at her own tears.

I followed her down the long hallway and out the doors of the house, making our way down the candlelit pathway that led to Hawk's parents' large garden. Hidden among formal hedges and rows of rose bushes, I caught sight of Emerson, my mini-me, flowers and braids holding up her silky hair, walking down the aisle with a basket of flower petals. Milo followed her on fat little legs, a handsome bow tie around his neck, sniffing at every petal she dropped.

They were the sweetest thing I'd ever seen.

That little girl was my dream come true, and so was her daddy, standing with a barely hidden smile on his face and waiting for me. Right under that giant oak tree we'd first kissed under so many years ago. We'd come a long way since then, and I wouldn't change a minute of it.

Mom squeezed my hand once then slid into her seat, tears still trickling down her face. Then the music started.

And I took the first step into my future with Hawk.

Our future together.

Our forever.

* * *

"Think they'll notice if we sneak away?" I breathed at his neck.

His hands were around me on the dance floor, the ceremony over, pictures finished, reception close to wrapping up.

"Do you think I give a shit who notices?" His crooked grin lit his cheeks. "Your tits look amazing. Ready for round two?"

I squealed when his palms slid across my ass cheeks and squeezed.

"More than ready." I nipped at his earlobe. That was apparently all it took because his hand clutched at mine, and we disappeared into the shadows, around a hedge of fragrant flowers, and deeper into the garden.

As soon as we were out of earshot of the party behind us, I dropped to my knees, halting him in his tracks. I worked at the belt and zipper of his pants quickly, freeing his heavy cock to the night air.

He sucked in a breath, hands in my elegant wedding hairstyle, mussing the curls and making me hotter for him. I cupped his thick shaft in my hand, stroking up the length and teasing the tip with my tongue. Slipping and sliding my tongue across the smooth flesh, I finally sucked the tip past my lips and tasted his arousal. A bead of pre-come on my tongue and my thighs were already damp with need.

"That's it, bury my cock in your throat, baby girl. Daddy needs to come." He grunted, hips thrusting into my throat, cock sliding past my tongue. "You looked so pretty up there saying 'I do' today. Took everything in me not to take you right there. I don't give a fuck who sees how much I love you."

He lifted me off the ground, hands pushing up the fabric of my dress and hooking into my panties. He dragged them down my legs in one swift movement, his fingers connecting with my searing flesh in the next.

I moaned, hands clutching at his shoulders before he lifted me in his arms, holding me to him tightly and impaling me on his dick. He fucked me like he was desperate, starved without me, and I think I understood it because last night without him in bed next to me had felt like another form of hell too.

A single day without his touch was too much to bear.

"Made me the happiest man alive today, baby girl," he murmured, fingers digging into my waist as his teeth grazed my neck. "I can't wait to have my next hundred lifetimes with you. We'll have first dates and first kisses, more babies and more love. So much love, Morgan. You fill me up inside," he gritted out, legs going rigid just as long jets of come emptied into me. His hand pushed between my thighs and rubbed at my swollen clit, sending stars shooting behind my eyelids as another orgasm ripped through me.

Gasping for breath, sweaty from the humid night air and our bodies pressed together, I came down, draped around him and so completely in love.

Everything about this man was love.

"Jesus, I hate that we have to go back there. I want to unwrap you, take my time, and lick every inch of your skin."

"That sounds like heaven." I smiled, kissing his earlobe. "I can't believe I had two orgasms on my wedding day."

"Say thank you," he ordered, hand slipping between my thighs again. "Say thank you, and I'll make it three."

"Mmm," I hummed. "Thank you, Daddy."

His eyes darkened, gaze focused on my lips. "I want to fuck that smirk right off your face, baby girl."

"That might have to wait for the honeymoon."

"Not waiting that long," he huffed.

"How long? Where are we going?"

His grin deepened before he set me on my feet and caught my hand in his. "A yacht."

"*A yacht?*"

"On the Mediterranean."

"On the Mediterranean! I can't leave the baby for that long—"

"Only a week, baby. Got it all settled with your mom. We've got a private flight tonight, and I plan on getting real familiar with the mile-high club."

"Oh my God, Hawk."

"Say it again, baby."

I flipped him the bird, his laugh following closely behind me all the way out of the garden.

God, I loved that man.

I was his girl. Always had been, always would be.

He hadn't known it then, but from that first kiss under his parents' oak tree, I was his girl.

THE END

Printed in Great Britain
by Amazon